Madman in Manhattan

BOOK 21

**MARIANNE HERING
ILLUSTRATIONS BY DAVID HOHN
AND SERGIO CARIELLO**

TYNDALE

**FOCUS ON THE FAMILY • ADVENTURES IN ODYSSEY®
TYNDALE HOUSE PUBLISHERS, INC. • CAROL STREAM, ILLINOIS**

To Aiden W. for confirming my hunch that third graders can be passionate about Nikola Tesla. And to Nathan Hoobler and Dave Arnold for sparking the idea for this book.

Madman in Manhattan

© 2018 Focus on the Family. All rights reserved.

A Focus on the Family book published by Tyndale House Publishers, Inc., Carol Stream, Illinois 60188.

The Imagination Station, Adventures in Odyssey, and *Focus on the Family* and their accompanying logos and designs are federally registered trademarks of Focus on the Family, 8605 Explorer Drive, Colorado Springs, CO 80920.

TYNDALE and Tyndale's quill logo are registered trademarks of Tyndale House Publishers, Inc.

Cover design by Michael Heath | Magnus Creative

ISBN: 978-1-58997-944-4

For Library of Congress Cataloging-in-Publication Data for this title, visit http://www.loc.gov/help/contact-general.html.

For manufacturing information regarding this product, please call 1-800-323-9400.

For information about special discounts for bulk purchases, please contact Tyndale House Publishers at csresponse@tyndale.com, or call 1-800-323-9400.

Printed in the United States of America

24	23	22	21	20	19	18
7	6	5	4	3	2	1

Contents

Prologue

At Whit's End, a lightning storm zapped the Imagination Station's computer. Then the Imagination Station began to do strange things. It took the cousins to the wrong adventures. The machine also gave the wrong gifts.

Whit was gone. No one knew when he would be back. He did not answer e-mails or phone calls.

Eugene was in charge of the workshop. An older version of the Imagination Station was found. It looked like a Model T car. Whit had made it for government use.

The car had a special feature called *lockdown mode.* The cousins used this machine for their adventures. But it began to break down too. Eugene couldn't fix it without help.

At the end of book 20, *Inferno in Tokyo,* Eugene was still locked in a jail cell. He was in Little Rock, Arkansas, in the year 1874. He was using a laptop to communicate with the cousins.

He sent them on a mission to find Nikola Tesla. But the broken Imagination Station took them to 1923 Tokyo, Japan, instead. There Patrick and Beth ended up helping people at the Imperial Hotel who survived a tsunami. Afterward, they were helping in the hotel kitchen. Here's what happened:

Each cousin wore an apron. Each was rolling rice balls.

"Four hundred thirty-three," Patrick said. He placed a ball on a tray.

"Four hundred thirty-four," Beth said. "Only nine thousand, five-hundred sixty-six more to go." She placed a rice ball on the tray.

Mr. Inumaru, the hotel manager, came through the side door of the kitchen. His kind face was split by a wide smile.

"You won't believe this," he said. "The US Navy sent you a gift. It was made in America. So they thought it belonged at the US embassy. But Mr. Kagawa said it belongs to you. So they put it on the garden patio. Come outside."

Beth and Patrick took off their aprons.

Patrick beat Beth to the patio. He was stunned.

Beth joined him. She took his hand and squeezed it.

"It's the Imagination Station!" she cried.

The Model T Imagination Station was covered in sand and seaweed. The driver's-side door was dented. The glass in the back was cracked in a spider-web design.

Beth's heart sank when she remembered it was broken.

Mr. Inumaru took a cloth out of his pocket. He began to wipe down the old car.

"It doesn't have any battery power left," Patrick said. "It's useless."

"Have you tried cranking it up?" Mr. Inumaru asked.

Beth shook her head.

Mr. Inumaru went to the front of the car. He

bent over and grabbed the crank. He turned it several times.

Suddenly a light came on inside the machine. Then a great burst of light exploded from the headlights.

Beth put her arm across her eyes to shield them from the brightness.

Mr. Inumaru shouted, "What? It can't be!"

Beth looked at the Model T.

Inside sat a man. He was waving the electric gizmo that Patrick and Beth had found in Babylon. It looked like a big TV remote control.

The man had thick, dark hair and a thick moustache. He wore a nice suit with a white shirt. He had a smug expression on his face.

"It's Mr. Tesla!" Mr. Inumaru said.

Mr. Tesla

Patrick rushed toward the Model T Imagination Station. He grabbed the passenger's-side handle and yanked the door open. A few gallons of ocean water poured onto the patio. The water splashed over his black shoes.

Old-fashioned dance music blared from the car's speakers.

Tesla looked at the yellow gizmo. "We're losing power," he said. "Mr. Inumaru, turn the hand crank!"

Mr. Inumaru said, "As you wish, Mr. Tesla. It's nice to see you again. I miss the old days when we both lived in New York. Your science experiments were the talk of the town!"

Mr. Inumaru grabbed the handle and turned the crank.

"Beth, get inside!" Patrick said.

Beth poked her head inside the machine. "Eww," she said, "there's seaweed on my seat."

She picked up a gray piece and tossed it into the bushes. Then she sat down.

Patrick turned to Tesla and said, "Eugene sent us to find you. He said you were the only one who could get us all back to our home."

Tesla squinted at Patrick. "Your home?" Tesla said. "I don't want to go to *your* home. I want to transport us to *my* home in Serbia. That's what this contraption does, correct?"

Beth and Patrick looked at each other. *Why*

had Eugene thought Mr. Tesla could help us? Patrick wondered.

Just then, the dance music on the speakers stopped. A familiar voice came over the speakers. "Patrick! Beth!"

Patrick recognized Eugene's voice! But he sounded a little strange.

"I forgot to tell you something very important," Eugene said. "Whatever you do, don't allow Mr. Tesla to use the Imagination Station itself. Who knows what trouble he could cause if he—"

Suddenly, Tesla banged on the control panel three times with his fist. The speakers crackled. Eugene's voice stopped. Patrick wondered if the speaker had been broken.

"What is that voice?" asked Tesla. "And what is an Imagination Station?"

Beth quickly motioned to her cousin. "Come

on, Patrick," she said. "We can squeeze in three."

Patrick shook his head. "The Imagination Station might not work with more than two inside," he whispered. "You go. Take Mr. Tesla back to New York. It's where he belongs."

Suddenly the Model T Imagination Station's headlights flickered and then blazed again.

Patrick stuck his head inside the car. "Reach over and turn the steering wheel," he whispered to Beth. "Get Mr. Tesla home. Maybe you'll learn why Eugene wanted us to find him. Then come back for me."

Beth nodded slowly. Patrick slammed the door shut.

Beth waved good-bye to Mr. Inumaru and Patrick. Then she grabbed the steering wheel. She spun it counterclockwise.

Patrick and Mr. Inumaru took a step backward. The car began to glow. The windshield filled with color. It looked like a kaleidoscope.

It took only a second for the Model T to vanish.

Beth and Tesla vanished along with it.

Manhattan

Beth opened her eyes. The Imagination Station had landed on top of a large, tall building. She opened the passenger's-side door. A bird instantly flew inside.

The bird's white wings flapped. Feathers flew.

Beth waved her arms and said, "Shoo!"

The flurry of flapping stopped. The bird settled on Tesla's shoulder. Beth could now see it was a white pigeon with gray wings.

The bird gently pecked at Tesla's ear. It seemed to be saying hello.

"Welcome, little beauty," Tesla said to the pigeon.

Beth studied the scientist now that he was in the sunlight. Tesla's hair was dark with flecks of gray. He had many fine wrinkles on his face. He still looked fit

and trim even though he was older.

The scientist reached inside his jacket pocket. He pulled out some birdseed and held it in his open palm. The pigeon pecked and ate the small yellow seeds.

Beth climbed out of the Model T.

Tesla got out of the Imagination Station too. He shut the driver's-side door. Then he opened and closed it two more times.

Beth wondered why the scientist closed the door three times. But she thought it would be rude to ask. So she kept quiet.

Next, Tesla tossed the rest of the birdseed on the ground. The bird flew off his shoulder to follow the seeds. A dozen more pigeons descended on the food and began pecking too. Their soft cooing was soothing.

Beth looked around the rooftop. At one end was a tarp that covered a large object. She thought perhaps it was an old air-conditioning unit.

Next she studied the city skyline. Many nearby buildings were taller than the one where she was. They also had spires on top.

Beth could see a wide river flowing a few blocks away. Boats chugged along the water. White clouds billowed from their stacks.

"The city is beautiful," Beth said.

"Welcome to Manhattan," Tesla said. He swept his arm as if to show off the city.

Beth was confused. "Mr. Inumaru said you lived in New York," she said.

"Manhattan Island is only one section of New York City. In 1898 the city became larger. It spread out over four other areas," Tesla said. "That was well before you were born."

Beth thought, *And even before my great-grandparents were born!*

She said, "Oh yeah. How could I forget that?" She extended a hand to Tesla in greeting. "I already know who you are. My name is Beth."

The scientist took a step backward. He pulled his hands close to his body and wrung them together.

"Excuse me," he said. "I cannot shake your hand. I injured mine not long ago in a laboratory accident."

"Did you burn them?" Beth asked. She took

a step toward him. "Let me take a look. Do you need a doctor?"

Tesla stuffed both hands in his pants pockets. "Oh no," he said. He backed farther away. "But your concern is noted."

Beth looked at the Imagination Station. Its cracked windows made her sad. But she noticed it hadn't vanished as it normally did.

She was curious how Tesla and the other in Tokyo could see it. And how he had appeared in the car in the first place. Usually the Imagination Station was invisible to everyone except Patrick and her.

"How did you get inside the . . . Model T to begin with?" Beth asked. After Eugene's warning, she thought it best not to call it the Imagination Station.

"I was standing on the roof," Tesla said. "Right where the car is now. It appeared in a transparent form. I walked toward it and touched the windshield . . ."

"And then what?" Beth asked. "Did you recognize the machine?"

Tesla nodded. "I think I've worked on something like it, but it was years ago," he said. "I got inside and opened the glove box. The yellow meter was there. There was also a panel for putting in coordinates for longitude and latitude. I quickly decided it must be some sort of transporter. So I put in the coordinates for Serbia and turned the steering wheel. I don't remember anything else until I saw you in Japan."

Beth wondered about the roof in Manhattan. Maybe it was a portal for the Imagination Station.

"My friend Eugene Meltsner said you can help us. He must think you can fix this . . . umm . . . this transporter machine," Beth said. She didn't think Tesla should know it could move through time. "You must be somebody special."

Tesla frowned. "I used to be," he said. "But in New York you have to be smart *and rich* to be somebody. Another inventor, Mr. Edison, squeezed me out of my fortune."

"Thomas Edison?" Beth said. "The man who invented the lightbulb?"

"Yes," Tesla said, "but *my* alternating-current system powers the lights! I invented it. Nearly every light in the city runs because of my electric generators."

Beth scratched her head. "Then you *should* be rich," she said.

Tesla raised a hand to his temple as if in despair. He said, "I had to give my patent to Mr. Westinghouse, my investor. Thomas Edison nearly bankrupted him, too. Edison is a good businessman. I am not."

Just then the Imagination Station's headlights

flashed and went out. Next the car's speakers let out a blast of static. Then they went silent.

"The transporter machine isn't working correctly," Beth said. "I'd like your help repairing it so I can get back to Eugene. Or else he'll spend the rest of his life in an Arkansas jail."

"You say this Eugene is a criminal?" Tesla asked.

Beth sighed. "He's in jail," she said. "But it's all a mistake. He works for Mr. Whittaker."

"Ah! There's a name I haven't heard in years," Tesla said and smiled.

Beth was surprised that Tesla had heard of Mr. Whittaker. How would someone in 1923 know him?

Then Tesla's moustache twitched. He looked like a contented cat that had just caught a mouse.

"I remember now. Of course you need my

help repairing the transporter machine," he said. "I'm the one who invented it."

Beth gasped. "That can't be true!" she said. "I know for a fact Mr. Whittaker built it. I found it in *his* workshop."

Tesla said, "John Avery Whittaker is another scoundrel. He must have stolen my patents for the cosmic induction generator. That's what powers this transporter machine."

"I can't believe that," Beth said. "Mr. Whittaker would never steal."

"Well, then explain this," Tesla said. He walked over to the Imagination Station and opened the hood.

Beth looked at the engine. It was made with electrical coils and rectangular metal grids.

On top of the largest coil was a small metal plate. The words on the plate said Tesla Electric Light & Manufacturing. Then the scientist took the yellow electronic gizmo out of his pocket. The meter lit up. A red light flashed.

"Is that a voltage meter?" Beth asked.

Tesla shook his head. "It measures radiation. This engine is powered by cosmic radiation converted to electric current."

Beth remembered her adventure in Babylon. "The meter lit up when I was near a lightning strike," she said.

"Exactly," Tesla said. "I'm trying to harness energy from the atmosphere. I mean I *have* harnessed it and turned it into electricity."

Beth didn't understand what the inventor was talking about. But she did know Whit hadn't stolen anything.

"I have the patents," Tesla said. "I filed one of them more than twenty years ago."

"So you can help us fix it?" Beth said. Hope welled up inside her.

"Of course I can," Tesla said. He slammed the car hood shut with a loud bang. "But only after I prove to you that I invented it!"

Martians

Mr. Inumaru turned to Patrick and said, "I hope your cousin is safe." Then the hotel manager walked from the garden patio to the kitchen.

The man's words made Patrick feel nervous. He followed Mr. Inumaru inside. "What do you mean?" Patrick asked.

"Mr. Tesla is a genius," Mr. Inumaru said. "But he's got some weird ideas."

"How weird?" Patrick asked. He felt his throat tighten with worry.

"Well, he's been trying to communicate with other planets," Mr. Inumaru said. "He built a 187-foot tower with a wireless transmitter on top. The total height of the tower was 225 feet! He also said he was sending signals to Mars. I feared the Martians would invade the city."

Patrick sighed and grinned. *Only Martians.* He felt better. Aliens wouldn't harm Beth.

Patrick stood at the kitchen table and began to roll rice balls again. Number 435.

The hotel manager turned to leave. Then he paused inside the kitchen doorway. "Mr. Tesla's lab is the real danger," Mr. Inumaru said.

"*Real* danger?" Patrick asked. He looked up from his work.

Mr. Inumaru added, "Something always sparks and burns when Mr. Tesla sets to work. His first lab burned down in 1895. He shocked himself once and passed out. He woke up and said he saw the past, present, and future. He said he could travel through time."

Sparks? Shocks? Now those were things to worry about. But three words worried Patrick more: "travel through time."

He wondered, *How did Mr. Tesla get inside the Imagination Station?*

The Elevator

"Follow me," Tesla said to Beth. "The copies of my US patents should be in my office."

Beth started to protest. "Really, you don't have to—"

"Oh, but I do," he said. "Someone is trying to steal my work. I need proof it's mine."

Tesla led the way to the edge of the roof. He walked like a proud man. His back was straight. His shiny black shoes made quick, sure movements.

Beth saw a ladder not too far away. It went straight down the side of the building. The metal rungs led to a fire-escape landing several floors down.

Tesla climbed down the ladder.

Beth gulped when she saw how high above the ground they were. Then she followed. She made sure her hands held firmly and her feet landed squarely on each rung.

Tesla stopped at the eighth-floor landing and opened the door. Then he shut it again.

Beth waited calmly as the scientist opened and closed the door again. He opened and closed it a third time. Then he held the door open. Beth shrugged and followed Tesla down a hallway.

The hotel carpet was white with large gold flowers. Small chandeliers with crystals and gold filigree hung from the ceiling.

Tesla passed a door marked Utility Room.

He paused at the service elevator. Then he flipped a lever on the wall.

Beth heard gears grinding. The elevator shaft was the size of a small garden shed. She could see it through the metal gate-like door. Beth thought the open hole looked dangerous.

She peered down the shaft and saw long, thick cables. She saw gears the size of trash-can lids. The elevator was coming toward them.

The elevator stopped at their floor. Beth noticed it didn't have a ceiling.

Tesla unlatched a lever that held the gate closed. He slid it to the side. The gate folded like an accordion.

Beth stepped inside.

On the elevator wall was a large, round, gold-colored crank.

"Which floor?" Beth asked.

"The third floor, please," Tesla said. He entered the elevator and slid the gate closed.

Then he locked the latch, unlocked it, and then locked it again. He did this one more time.

Beth waited until Tesla finished. Then she pressed the elevator button with the number three on it.

Tesla turned the crank. The elevator began to descend.

"Cool," Beth said. "I've never been in an elevator like this!" She looked at Tesla. "Did you invent this, too?"

The scientist's face turned red. "I did not," Tesla said. "My invention would have been completely electric. No manual cranks or levers."

They rode the rest of the way in silence.

The elevator stopped at the third floor. Tesla opened the gate.

Beth stepped out. "Which way to your room?" she asked Tesla.

"Left and then left again," he said. He fiddled with his moustache.

She followed the scientist to a large white door. The brass plate on it read 333.

Beth walked inside the suite. It was filled with metal parts, tools, and weird electrical coils. Some of the coils were tall enough to touch the ceiling. This room was obviously a lab and not an office. It reminded Beth of Whit's workshop.

Tesla headed straight to a small window. Beth could see a pigeon perched on the ledge. It pecked at the glass pane.

Tesla tapped on the glass three times. Then he opened the window. The bird hopped inside. "Hello again, little beauty," he said to the pigeon.

Is that the same bird that landed on Mr. Tesla's shoulder? Beth wondered. It was white with some gray wing feathers.

Beth looked around for filing cabinets that might hold the patent papers.

The adjoining door to the rest of the suite was open. Beth peered inside. It was an office and a bedroom. It had a telephone, a telegraph machine, and one small filing cabinet.

An older, African-American boy was inside. He wore a white shirt and an orange bow tie. He was sitting at a wood desk with a large writing surface. The desktop tilted so the boy could write on it easily. It looked as if he was drawing.

"Are your patent files in the other suite?" Beth asked the scientist.

Tesla went to the door to the adjoining room. "Gerald Norman," he called.

The boy stood. "Yes, sir?"

"This is Beth," Tesla said. "She's a friend of the inventor John Whittaker."

Gerald nodded.

Tesla said, "Bring me the records for the cosmic radiation converter."

A frown flashed across Gerald's face. "I can't, sir," he said. "They aren't here."

"Lost?" Tesla said.

"No, sir," Gerald said. "They were left behind at the Wardenclyffe lab when it closed down."

"You mean when my tower was destroyed. At least the lab building is still standing," Tesla said. Then his face turned red.

"Millionaire J. P. Morgan stopped funding my experiments," he said to Beth. "He stopped believing in me. I watched dynamite blow up my life's work. My creditors sold the scrap metal to pay back my debts."

"What was your life's work?" Beth asked.

"A transmitter tower," Tesla said. "It was designed to broadcast signals around the world without wires."

"Oh," Beth said. "Like a cell-phone tower that relays radio fre—" She stopped short. She remembered too late that she was in the 1920s. Cell phones wouldn't be invented for at least fifty years.

Tesla's eyes narrowed to a squint. "You've been snooping through my notes," he said. The scientist pointed at her. "Who sent you to spy on me?"

"No one," Beth said. "Don't you remember? You showed up in Tokyo and brought me here."

Gerald gave a little cough. Beth and Tesla turned toward him.

The boy was holding a large piece of paper. "Did I get the landing system right?"

Beth looked at the drawing. It showed a helicopter-like contraption. The sketch was amazingly detailed.

"Wow," Beth said. "You're good. Who taught you to be a draftsman?"

"My grandfather," Gerald said. "Lewis Latimer."

"His grandfather used to work for Thomas Edison!" Tesla said. His face had a sour expression.

"You don't have to hire me, Mr. Tesla," the boy said. "I can find work with someone else."

"No, no," Tesla said. "Your grandfather trained you well. Lewis Latimer has always been an honest man and a good patent consultant."

Tesla smiled. "He helped Alexander Graham Bell get the patent for the telephone. Latimer filed the patent with only two hours to spare. The competitor got to the patent office too late. That story is legend."

Gerald said, "Then go see my grandfather. You can trust him. He has copies of your patents. They're at the law firm of Hammer and Schwarz."

"Ahh!" Tesla said. "Edwin Hammer is a Thomas Edison fan. I wonder if he let Edison see my patent for the transporter machine."

"Would that be bad?" Beth asked.

Tesla smiled. "If Thomas Edison likes the

ideas," he said, "he might fund the project." Then his smile turned upside down into a frown. "Or he could see something I missed and create a new patent."

Tesla motioned to Beth to follow him to the door. "Come on," he said. "Let's get those patents. I want to protect my rights."

Beth headed toward the door. She passed a bookshelf. A Bible sat on one of the shelves.

"Do you believe in God?" she asked Tesla.

"Hmm," he said. "My mother did." He pointed to the Bible. "She gave me that when I was a boy."

"Do you read it?" Beth asked.

"Not often," Tesla said. "But the passages about lightning in the book of Revelation are fascinating. And I believe God created the world with enough power for our needs. That power can be harnessed for our good."

Beth looked hesitant. "But the Bible isn't just a book about electricity. It tells about

God's power in all things. And how He wants people to give Him credit for it."

"I know something about the Bible," Tesla said. "The ninth commandment says not to lie or bear false witness. The Model T transporter machine is my invention. I'm an honorable scientist. You'll see I'm telling the truth!"

Mr. Meltsner

Patrick was alone in the kitchen of the Imperial Hotel. He was on rice ball number 602. He heard a low humming noise. He wondered what it was.

Patrick moved in the direction of the sound. It was coming from the garden patio. He went outside.

The white, modern Imagination Station

39

appeared. It was in the exact place the car Imagination Station had stood. An old man in a suit with a bow tie sat in the car. He waved when he saw Patrick.

The old man got out of the machine slowly. His shoulders slouched. He had on round, wire-rimmed glasses.

"Greetings, Patrick!" the old man said.

His voice seemed strangely familiar to Patrick.

"Who are you?" Patrick asked.

The man smiled. He said, "Who else? I am none other than your old friend Eugene Meltsner!" The man took a couple of steps toward Patrick.

Patrick's eyes opened in surprise. "You really *are* old!" Patrick said. "And your hair is white!"

Eugene spread his arms wide. He started to shuffle toward Patrick. "Kindly don't force me to walk all the way to you," Eugene said.

Patrick stepped forward and gave his friend a hug.

"You walk slowly. And you kind of stoop now too," Patrick said. "Should I call you Mr. Meltsner?"

Eugene laughed. "It would seem appropriate," he said. "It's been forty-nine years since you saw me in the jail cell."

Patrick scrunched his eyebrows. "We've never aged in an adventure before," he said. "You're much older, but I'm not. What happened?"

"It's a lengthy narrative," Eugene said. "I'll tell it to you once we find Beth. She should be with Nikola Tesla in Manhattan. That's what my computer says. I've been waiting for you two to appear in my time line."

"How did you know I was here?" Patrick said. "The tsunami from the Tokyo earthquake interrupted our trip to New York."

"I was able to trace the Model T Imagination Station's movements," Eugene said. "I still have my laptop and figured out how to charge it. As soon as I saw the Model T land here, I attempted to communicate with you to give you the message about Mr. Tesla. Did you hear it?"

"Part of it," said Patrick. "But Mr. Tesla hit the controls while you were talking. I think he might have broken the speakers. All we heard was that we needed his help. But we shouldn't let him use the machine. Since he was already in it, we figured Beth should take him back to New York."

"Ah," muttered Eugene. "Now it all makes sense."

The Imagination Station started to make a low humming sound.

"It's time to go," Eugene said. He motioned toward the modern Imagination Station. "Mr. Tesla has access to the Model T Imagination Station. We have to make sure he doesn't keep it too long or . . ."

"Or what?" Patrick asked.

"I shudder to think of it," Eugene said. "Nikola Tesla is one of the most brilliant men who ever lived. But he won't understand the power source Mr. Whittaker invented. It could blow up if Tesla tinkers with it."

"Can't we go back to Whit's End and fix the machines there?" Patrick asked. "I don't trust either of the Imagination Stations."

Eugene shook his head. "I'm sorry," he said. "The machines will stay in 1923 until they're repaired. We can travel to *places*, but we can't travel to a specific *year*."

Patrick heard voices coming from the hotel grounds. "Will anyone be able to see us leave?" he asked.

"Unfortunately yes," Eugene said. "Everyone in 1923 will be able to see the machine appear and disappear. It's a minor glitch, if you will. Nothing really when you consider the risks I've taken."

"Risks? What risks?" Patrick asked.

"I needn't get into all of them now. One was coming here where everyone can see us," Eugene said. "Let's depart before someone comes and asks what we're doing."

Patrick helped Eugene get inside the Imagination Station. Then Patrick climbed into the machine and shut the door.

"I wish I could say good-bye to Mr. Inumaru," Patrick said. "I'll be gone when he gets back to the kitchen. He might think I ran away from my job rolling rice balls. I had 9,398 left to make."

"You can write him a letter," Eugene said. "They do have mail in 1923."

Patrick settled into the comfortable seat. He looked at the dashboard. The red button in the middle was flashing. He pushed it.

The Imagination Station started to shake. Then it rumbled. It seemed to move forward. Patrick shut his eyes. It felt like a roller coaster out of control.

The machine whirled.

Suddenly everything went black.

Lewis Latimer

Beth and Tesla came downstairs on the guest elevator. Beth said a cheerful good-bye to the doorman. Then she and the scientist left the Hotel Marguery just past noon. They walked along Park Avenue to the law offices of Hammer and Schwarz.

Small trees lined the sidewalk. They were ablaze with fall colors. A few red leaves floated like little kites in the wind.

Red streetcars glided along tracks in the

street. Yellow taxis and large black cars wove in and out of traffic. Newspaper boys darted along the sidewalks in knickers and caps. Men wearing dark suits and hats hurried to appointments.

A few women also walked along Park Avenue. Beth thought their dresses were pretty with their bows and fringe. She knew the young ladies were called flappers. Their hats were small and fit tightly on their heads.

Tesla often stopped walking to feed pigeons. Or sometimes he ducked inside a stone doorway and hid. He would stand there with his face against the door for a moment. Then he would look over his shoulder and begin walking again.

"Why are you dodging into the doorways?" Beth asked when he ducked into a doorway again. "What are you hiding from?"

"I don't like to look at a woman wearing pearls," Tesla said. "I have to hide my eyes till she passes by."

Beth's mouth dropped open. Pearls were in fashion in the 1920s. Many women wore several long strands around their necks.

"And I especially don't like pearl earrings," he said. He tipped his hat in Beth's direction. "I'm glad you don't wear jewelry."

Then Tesla started walking down the sidewalk again. The heels of his shiny black shoes softly thudded on the pavement.

Suddenly there was a flapping of wings. The same white pigeon as before landed on Tesla's shoulder. He walked on as if that weren't unusual.

Beth had to hurry to keep up.

Tesla stopped in front of a door in a tall gray

office building. The bird flew off his shoulder. It perched on a nearby bush.

Beth liked the small stained-glass panel at the top of the door. A brass plaque below the window read *Hammer and Schwarz, Patent Attorneys.*

The scientist grabbed the handle and pushed the door open. A bell above the door jingled. Then Tesla closed and opened the door twice more.

Tesla went inside. Beth followed.

The office was cozy. The carpet had a rose design. There was an umbrella holder with two black umbrellas. A weird-looking rack stood in the corner behind the door. A coat hung from it.

A long wood counter blocked them from going farther inside. On the counter was a little brass bell. The handle was carved in the shape of a bulldog's head.

Tesla picked up the bell and rang it three times.

An old African-American man appeared from somewhere in the back of the office. His skin was the color of light caramel. The hair at his temples was completely gray. He wore round, wire-rimmed glasses.

"Why, it's my old friend Nikola Tesla!" the man said. "Good day!" He reached over the counter. He offered his hand to Tesla.

"Hello, Lewis," Tesla said. "Excuse me. I cannot shake your hand."

Beth winked at Latimer. "He burned his hands in a lab accident not long ago," she said. "He doesn't need to see a doctor."

Tesla said, "Exactly."

Latimer winked back at Beth. She had a feeling he understood Mr. Tesla's dislike of touching people.

Latimer changed the subject. He said, "I see you have a new companion."

"This is a new friend, Beth," Tesla said.

The man beamed a smile. "I'm Lewis Latimer," he said. "Nikola and I had the honor of working for Mr. Edison. And we both worked on improving and installing streetlights."

"But I lost the patents on that, too," Tesla said. "Edison didn't want to invest in my idea. I had to turn the patents over to another company. And they also chose not to put money behind my idea."

"It's a tough business being an inventor," Latimer said. He held out his hand to Beth and said, "It's a pleasure to meet you."

Beth took the offered hand and shook it.

"I'm here to make sure no one is using my patents without permission," Tesla said. "The two important ones are 787,412 and 685,957. They're for converting cosmic radiation into electric current and basic energy transfer."

"Of course," Latimer said. "I researched those

patents just this week for three gentlemen. One was Mr. Edison." He moved some papers around on the counter. "Here they are," he said. He pushed the stack of papers toward Tesla.

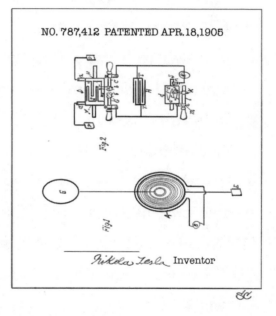

NO. 787,412 PATENTED APR. 18, 1905

Nikola Tesla Inventor

"You said Edison was interested in my radiation power source?" Tesla cried. "I don't want him looking into this. At least not until I can show him it works. And it does! I've got a working model!"

Beth knew Tesla was referring to the Imagination Station. But she also knew it was Mr. Whittaker's invention. She said, "Mr. Whittaker made it work. Don't forget him."

Latimer said, "I haven't seen Mr. Whittaker for years. What happened to that pleasant inventor?"

Beth was surprised. How many people in 1923 knew Whit? But she really couldn't explain where he was. So she said, "Oh, he gets around. I see him here and there."

"Tell him I said hello," Latimer said.

Beth nodded.

Tesla looked through the papers. Then he turned pale as sour cream. He asked Latimer, "Do you think Edison would steal my ideas? I don't have the money to fight him in court. He would win."

Latimer raised his hands, palms out. It seemed like a gesture to keep Tesla calm.

"Edison did not see the details of your design," Latimer said. "He was making sure his new patent didn't copy your ideas. We're paid to protect your ideas, not help others steal them."

"Ha!" Tesla said. "I've never been protected by the lawyers or the courts."

"You're referring to the Marconi incident?" Latimer asked.

"Yes," Tesla said. "That scoundrel won a Nobel Prize for my patent on wireless radio."

Beth was shocked. "Really?" she said. She looked at Latimer for an explanation.

Latimer sighed and said, "Mr. Marconi was working on radio in England. At the same time, Mr. Tesla was working on it in America. But Mr. Tesla's lab burned down. He lost his research."

Beth looked at Mr. Tesla. His shoulders slumped, and his eyes seemed dull. He suddenly looked tired and hopeless.

Latimer added, "Mr. Tesla did have the first patents. But Mr. Marconi had money to continue researching. Mr. Marconi was the first to present wireless radio to the world.

And then Mr. Edison and others invested in Mr. Marconi's company."

Beth thought, *Another reason Mr. Tesla might not like Mr. Edison.* Then she said, "What happened next?"

Tesla said, "The courts gave Mr. Marconi rights to the radio patents in 1904. Several years later he won the Nobel Prize. The world doesn't know that I, Nikola Tesla, invented radio."

Beth wanted to put a hand on the inventor's arm. But instead she said, "I'm sorry."

Tesla placed his hand on the counter. Beth could see it was shaking with emotion.

"I don't want another patent stolen," Tesla said. "Who else wanted to see my radiation converter plans?"

"Henry Ford is looking to make an affordable electric car," Latimer said. "He wants to eliminate the need for charging stations. He and I discussed many alternative sources of power."

"Do you like Mr. Ford?" Beth asked Tesla. "Why don't you work—"

Beth stopped talking when she saw the expression on Tesla's face. It had turned into a fierce scowl.

"Ford is Edison's best friend!" Tesla said. "Those two work only with each other. They would never include me in their inventions."

Beth shrank back. Again she said she was sorry. The list of people Tesla had disagreements with was getting longer. Beth silently listed them: *Mr. Edison, Mr. Whittaker, Mr. Morgan, Mr. Marconi, and now Mr. Ford.*

Latimer coughed politely. Beth thought he wanted to change the subject.

Latimer pulled out a large black book. He opened it flat on the desk.

Beth could see the book had two columns.

The first was filled with names. The second was filled with numbers.

"Let me see who the third gentleman was," Latimer said. He dragged a finger down the names column.

"Ah yes," Latimer said. "Here we go . . . The last name starts with *M*. But the handwriting is a bit messy. I can't read it properly." He reached behind the counter and pulled out a magnifying glass.

Tesla looked defeated. "Tell me, was it *M* for Marconi? I need to know."

Latimer said, "No, Marconi's first name starts with a *G*." He held up the magnifying glass and studied the page. "The first initial here is clearly an *E*. The last name is Mel—

"Meltsner!" Beth shouted. "Eugene Meltsner was here!"

"Yes, I remember that white-haired gentleman now," Latimer said. "A very curious older fellow. He was engaging and definitely rich. He asked me all about Nikola's inventions. Especially about the transmitter and harnessing energy from the atmosphere."

Latimer turned to Tesla and smiled. "Perhaps you should meet him. He might lend you money to build a new invention."

Suddenly Tesla's eyes narrowed. He looked at Beth. "Isn't this Eugene Meltsner your friend in Arkansas?"

"Yes, but . . . I don't understand," Beth said. She leaned across the counter to look Latimer in the eye. She asked, "Did you say he had white hair and was old?"

Latimer nodded. "Older than I am. And I turn seventy-five tomorrow."

"The Eugene I know is a young man," Beth said. "He has red hair."

Tesla slammed his palm on the counter again. "I knew it!" he shouted. "This Eugene fellow was wearing a disguise. He's a spy for John Whittaker."

Beth silently added Eugene Meltsner to Tesla's list of enemies. *Who will be next?* she wondered.

Tesla turned toward Beth. He pointed a long, thin finger at her. "And you're a spy too!"

The Long Island Lab

Patrick opened his eyes.

The white Imagination Station had landed. It stood in front of a long, single-story brick building. A small tower jutted from the top.

Weeds grew around the building in sandy areas. Lumber and rusted wire fencing lay in piles not far away.

Eugene said, "We've arrived at Wardenclyffe, Tesla's abandoned lab."

Patrick opened the door of the Imagination

Station and got out. Then he helped Eugene out of the machine.

"What now?" Patrick asked his old friend.

"Let's go inside," Eugene said. "I want to show you something. Then we'll go find Beth and Mr. Tesla."

Patrick helped Eugene walk to the door. Eugene pulled a key out of his pocket and unlocked the door.

Patrick stepped inside the lab. It was too dark to see much. Black paper covered the inside of the windows.

"Allow me to turn on the lights," Eugene said. "But first I must close the door. I don't want anyone to see in. It's important that everyone think this building is empty."

Patrick heard the door close and then a soft click. The room instantly filled with light.

Patrick looked around. He whistled and said, "This is amazing!"

Inside the building was an enormous workshop. There were lots of electric contraptions, coils, cylinders, and small towers. Scattered everywhere were car parts, helicopter parts, wire antennas, and small motors. Hundreds of mechanical drawings on paper were pinned to the walls.

Patrick slowly walked around the room. He touched what looked like a giant crystal ball. Suddenly his hair stood on end.

"Use extreme caution," Eugene said. "You can shoot bolts of electricity from that one."

Patrick remembered Mr. Inumaru's warning about the dangers of Tesla's lab. He quickly removed his hand.

"Go stand in the center of the lab," Eugene said. "And then rub your hands together vigorously."

"Is it safe?" Patrick asked.

Eugene laughed. "We're in Nikola Tesla's

lab. Not even he would be totally safe here," he said. He chuckled and then added, "But this experiment is harmless. I've done it hundreds of times."

Patrick did as he was told. He stood in the middle of the floor. He rubbed his hands together. Then he opened them. Suddenly a cloud of swirling electricity appeared on each of his palms.

Patrick was too stunned to say or do anything.

But Eugene clapped slowly. "Well done, Wizard Patrick," he said.

Patrick moved from the center of the room. The electricity disappeared. He shook his head in amazement.

"Where did you get all this stuff?" Patrick asked.

"Tesla's lab was shut down six years ago," Eugene said. "It's taken me since then to

slowly rebuild it. I buy pieces wherever I can. Thankfully I have a good knowledge of history. That enables me to know where to find the resources I need."

"But why are you doing it?" Patrick asked.

"Because I need to know how to fix the Imagination Stations," Eugene said. "That's why I sent you to find Mr. Tesla in the first place. The answer is in one of his experiments. I've replicated them exactly. Except for three of them."

"Which three?" Patrick asked.

"In 1899 Mr. Tesla moved to Colorado and created a way to make lightning. That experiment drained the nearby electric company," Eugene said. "Out of an abundance of caution, I decided I wouldn't attempt that one. A million volts is significantly more than the Imagination Station could handle."

"A million!" Patrick said. "Wow!"

Eugene added, "And making a death ray wasn't going to be helpful either."

Patrick gulped. "Mr. Tesla made a death ray like the ones in comic books?"

Eugene nodded. "Thankfully it was impractical for military use. It never went into production."

"What was the last experiment?" Patrick asked.

"Mr. Tesla built a transmitter tower to send signals around the world. But the tower was torn down in 1917," Eugene said. "I couldn't possibly build a 225-foot structure without people noticing it. But that's the critical experiment. It's the key to fixing the Imagination Stations."

"Why?" Patrick asked.

Eugene shuffled over to a desk. He fumbled around till he found a file folder. He pulled out

Tesla Transmitter at Wardenclyffe Topples

picture by Sergio Cariello

a black-and-white newspaper. He laid it on the desk.

"This is what I wanted to show you," Eugene said. He tapped the corner of a photo on the front page and asked, "What do you see?"

Patrick squinted and stared at a group of men. They were watching as a giant wood tower toppled over. One of the men was Nikola Tesla. There was another familiar face too.

"It can't be," Patrick said.

"It is," Eugene said.

"How did Mr. Whittaker get in that photo?" Patrick asked.

Broken Glass

"Me? A spy?" Beth said to Tesla. "I'm still in elementary school."

Latimer said, "Really, Nikola, you're taking this too far. She's only a child."

Tesla merely scowled. He scooped the patent papers off the counter. He turned, opened the door, and left the offices of Hammer and Schwarz. The door slammed behind him.

The pretty stained glass in the door shook loose. It fell to the floor and shattered.

Beth bent to clean it up.

"Don't do that," Latimer said. "I'll sweep up the shards. You follow Mr. Tesla. He needs someone with him when he's angry."

Beth nodded. "Thank you, Mr. Latimer," she said. "You're kind."

Beth was careful to step around the glass. Then she hurried out the door to find Tesla.

She looked up and down the sidewalk for the unhappy inventor. She spotted him already a block away. It looked as if he was headed back to the Hotel Marguery.

Tesla walked at a fast pace. The patent papers were rolled up under one arm.

This time he hadn't opened and closed the law office door three times. And now he didn't stop to feed the pigeons. He didn't hide from women wearing pearls.

Beth had to jog to catch up with him. Her shoes hammered the sidewalk. Leaves crunched as she ran. She was fuming. *I am not a spy. I am not a spy,* she thought. She wondered if Tesla would ever help them fix the Imagination Station now. Perhaps her trip here would end in failure.

She looked at the skyline. She could see the Hotel Marguery up ahead.

A streetcar passed through the intersection in front of them. Tesla paused at the crosswalk at Forty-Eighth Street and Park Avenue. The white pigeon flew down and landed on his shoulder.

Beth caught up with the inventor at the curb. She still felt angry that he thought she was a spy.

"Why won't you trust me?" Beth asked him. "I'm not going to steal your ideas. I can't even read the long words in the patents you're carrying. And I haven't seen Mr. Whittaker in years."

It wasn't an outright lie. But it felt like a half truth. She added, "I mean, I haven't seen him for years in your time."

Tesla looked down at her. His piercing, dark eyes seemed to see into her soul.

"*My* time?" he asked. He held up two fingers. "So there are *two* times—mine and yours?"

Beth didn't answer. But her eyes grew round with panic. She'd said too much.

Suddenly the scientist smiled. "He did it!"

"Who did what?" Beth asked.

"John Avery Whittaker built a time machine," he said. "I thought he was a madman. *But he did it!*"

Tesla was practically tap-dancing with joy. He raised his arms into the air. "Whittaker did it!" he shouted and spun around. The movement frightened the pigeon. It flew away.

Beth said quietly, "It's not *exactly* a time machine. We call it the Imagination Station."

But the scientist didn't seem to hear her.

"That's what that voice meant in the machine! You wanted to prevent me from using this Imagination Station to travel through time, didn't you?" Tesla gave Beth a piercing glance.

"Not exactly," she said, unsure of how to explain.

"Quickly!" Tesla said. "We have to get to the roof of the Hotel Marguery. I must learn how the time machine works. Then I can turn in a patent! I'll do it before Edison and Ford even know it exists!"

The Photo

Patrick stared at the 1917 photo of Whit at Wardenclyffe. He blinked. He looked at the newspaper clipping again. Whit was still there. The photo showed the transmitter tower being taken down.

It all began to sink in. Patrick put together his jumbled thoughts.

"Mr. Whittaker knew Mr. Tesla," he said. "Mr. Whittaker built the first Imagination Station. He used Mr. Tesla's ideas and maybe even his help. So Mr. Tesla knows how to build an Imagination Station."

Eugene was quiet.

Patrick looked toward his friend and added, "But Mr. Tesla doesn't know he knows. Is that right?"

Patrick's second question was also met with silence.

Eugene was standing across the room. Now Patrick could hear faint clicking sounds. The noise was coming from a machine sitting on a wood table.

The machine looked half piano and half reel-to-reel movie projector. The row of piano-like keys had letters and numbers on them.

A narrow piece of paper was coming off a reel.

Eugene gently held the paper as it emerged. It was about as wide as the paper in a fortune cookie.

Patrick walked over to Eugene and stared

at the paper. He was expecting a code with dashes and dots. But the paper had words printed on it.

The message said, "EM, I told NT about you. The girl was here with him. He has the patents. He's headed to HM at a quarter to two. LL"

Patrick figured out that EM was Eugene Meltsner. NT must be Nikola Tesla. The girl had to be Beth.

He looked at a clock on the wall. It was nearly two o'clock. The telegram had taken only a few minutes to be routed.

"What does the HM stand for?" Patrick asked. "And who is LL?"

Eugene didn't answer. He flipped a switch on the machine. He pushed the piano-like keys to enter "On our way." The machine clicked for a few seconds. Then it fell silent.

Excitement lit up Eugene's expression.

Patrick thought his friend seemed a bit younger.

Eugene finally said, "HM stands for the Hotel Marguery. And LL is Lewis Latimer, a friend."

Eugene picked up his laptop off a nearby desk. He started to shuffle to the door. "I can't explain how long I've waited for this moment!" he cried. "Let's go meet Nikola Tesla! We'll take the Imagination Station to the roof portal."

"Isn't that risky?" Patrick asked.

"Not compared to the New York public transportation system," Eugene said.

Race to the Rooftop

Beth felt like sticking out her tongue at Tesla. But she knew that was too rude. Instead, she stomped her foot on the sidewalk and cried, "You said you invented the machine! You said you had the patents! You said you had honor!"

Tesla blushed. Beth wondered if he felt ashamed for lying.

"I helped Whittaker perfect the power system," Tesla said. "I didn't know the machine could enter another time dimension. That's the most fantastic invention ever created!"

Tesla looked at the sky. He raised his hands as if motioning to God. "We can change history!" he said. "I can get my patents back. I'll be rich! Thomas Edison will ask to work for me!"

Passersby stared at Tesla. They moved to the other side of the street.

Beth saw a wild gleam in Tesla's eyes. She wondered why Eugene had sent them to find this man in the first place. He was definitely a troublemaker. No good could come from a mad scientist traveling through history. She had to get to the rooftop before he did. She had to hide the Imagination Station.

"I'm going to stop you," she said. "You don't deserve to use that machine. Mr. Whittaker would never allow it."

The streetcar finished passing. Suddenly a nearby church bell rang twice. Beth burst into a sprint down Park Avenue. Her shoes slapped on the sidewalk. She ran so fast that her hair lifted and flapped in the wind.

She arrived at the hotel and scurried up the front steps. She dodged past the doorman and into the vast lobby. She passed under the gold chandeliers and raced by posh furniture. Up ahead was the guest elevator.

Three ladies were waiting for the elevator. Beth's heart sank. The elevator might stop once for each person. Three stops would take too long.

Beth couldn't make up her mind which way to go. Maybe the ladies all lived on the same floor. Maybe the elevator would be faster if there were only one stop.

Beth looked over her shoulder.

Tesla had entered the lobby. Their eyes met. He began to walk quickly toward her.

Beth decided she couldn't risk the elevator. She had to get to the roof before he did. She turned the hallway corner toward the stairwell. She paused. There were many floors to climb, and she was already out of breath.

The service elevator! Beth rushed toward the back of the hallway. She turned right and then right again.

It's on this floor! Beth quickly got inside the service elevator. She closed the interior metal folding gate. She pushed the button for floor eight. She knew that floor led to the roof ladder.

Beth looked through the gate. She saw Tesla round the corner. But he didn't come toward her. Instead, he opened the utility-room door. Then he closed it and opened it again.

Beth knew she had a few seconds. Tesla was going to open the door a total of three times. She put her hand on the gold crank. She started to turn it. She went up a couple of floors.

Suddenly the lights went out. The crank became harder to turn. She was in total darkness.

Tesla must have gone into the utility room and turned off the electricity! Beth fumed. *Oh, he is smart.*

Beth pictured him slowly walking up the stairs. Maybe he was even whistling a merry tune. Tesla would be in no hurry because he knew she was trapped.

Beth's heart sank. The elevator was creepy. How long would it be before someone found her?

"Think, Beth!" she said aloud.

Hadn't Tesla said the service elevator wasn't completely electric? Beth gripped the crank handle tightly. She pushed down on it with all her might. The crank and the elevator started to move.

As she got the crank going, the turning became easier. She heard something grinding. The system of gears, pulleys, and counterweights was working. Faster and faster she cranked. Faster and faster the elevator rose.

Then it suddenly stopped with a clank and a thud.

I must be on floor eight, Beth thought.

She felt for the metal gate. She found the lever, unlatched it, and opened the cage.

Then she stepped hesitantly into the darkness. Her foot found the floor. She put her hand on the wall and started walking. The wall helped guide her to the fire-escape landing. She opened the door.

She felt the autumn breeze as she stepped outside. The afternoon sunshine welcomed her.

She looked up at the ladder. No Tesla.

Beth breathed a sigh of relief. She grabbed a metal rung. She barely noticed the cold metal. She stepped onto the ladder and climbed quickly upward.

As she neared the top, she could see the roof clearly.

Beth gasped. She was too late. The Model T Imagination Station was gone!

The Missing Forty-Nine Years

The modern Imagination Station landed on the roof of the Hotel Marguery.

Patrick heard pounding. He saw a small hand come down on the windshield.

"Get out!" Beth shouted. "Get out! Someone stole the Model T Imagination Station!"

Beth moved to the side of the machine. She yanked the door open.

She grabbed Patrick's arm and tugged. "Come on!" she said. "We have to do something!"

Patrick staggered out onto the roof. He glanced at the city skyline. Then he noted the large object covered with a tarp. He thought it might be a storage unit for the janitor. He saw a dozen pigeons perched on the roof ledge.

"Patrick!" Beth said.

He took Beth's hand. "Are you all right?" he asked. "Where's Mr. Tesla?"

Beth looked at him. Her eyes were wide open with shock. "I am not all right. Didn't you hear what I said? *The Imagination Station is missing.*" She was breathing hard. "I have no idea where Mr. Tesla is. I think he stole the Imagination Station."

Suddenly Beth's eyes grew even larger. Her pupils shrank with fear. She was staring at something behind Patrick. What was it?

Patrick turned around. Eugene had

stepped out of the Imagination Station. He
was standing next to it. His laptop was in his
hands.

"Who is that?" Beth
said. "It looks like a wax
statue of Eugene. But it
melted."

Eugene waved.
"Greetings," he said. He
shuffled forward.

Beth rushed toward
him and hugged him
tight.

"Mr. Latimer was right," she said. "You
are old."

Eugene seemed to totter when she let go of
him. She took the laptop and held it under her
arm.

"Do you need to sit down?" she asked.

"Yes, I believe I must," Eugene said. He

shuffled to a little air-vent hood jutting up from the roof. It was the right height for a seat. He sat on it.

Beth handed Eugene the laptop. He lifted the cover. Then he opened a few programs and typed on the keyboard.

"I can't tell who took the machine," Eugene said. "The computer shows the Model T Imagination Station is at Wardenclyffe."

He keyed in something else. "It's locked now. No one can use it to leave. Whoever took it will have to exit immediately."

Beth sat next to Eugene and held his hand. "I still don't know how he beat me to the rooftop," she said. "He must be in great shape. He ran up eight floors faster than I traveled in the elevator. And I had a head start."

Patrick sat on the rooftop with his legs crossed. His chin rested on his palm.

Patrick said to Eugene, "Tell us what

happened to you. How did you get out of the Arkansas jail?"

Eugene coughed. "Well," he said. "It began on a dark and stormy night."

Beth groaned.

"It really did happen as the result of a storm," Eugene said. "Rain caused a flash flood. It loosened the ground. The bricks in the jailhouse shifted, opening a crack in the wall."

Patrick said, "And you clawed at the bricks with your bare hands. Then you escaped through a hole."

Eugene shook his head. "I had to disassemble the metal bed frame first. I used one of the rails as a crowbar and shifted the bricks to produce a hole."

Beth added, "And then you escaped through the hole."

Eugene shook his head. "I didn't have

the laptop," he said. "Mr. Pinkerton had it. I needed to wait till Detective Pinkerton trusted me. So I had to replace the bricks and reassemble the bed."

Patrick yawned. "Get to the good stuff," he said. "What did you do after you crawled through the hole?"

Eugene smiled. "I never crawled through the hole."

"What?" Beth asked. "Then how did you escape?"

"I didn't," Eugene said.

Beth groaned again. "Just tell us how it happened, please," she said.

Patrick saw her squeeze Eugene's hand.

Eugene sat up straighter. He seemed proud of himself. "I showed the hole to Detective Pinkerton."

Patrick was surprised. "That was brave," he said, "and perhaps not so smart."

Eugene smiled again. "Indeed, it was both. But it worked exactly as I had hoped. Detective Pinkerton saw I could be trusted, and he returned the laptop."

Beth giggled. "Then you crawled through the hole!" she said.

"I was set free," Eugene said. "It was much more satisfying. And I wasn't a fugitive."

Patrick said, "Okay, what happened during the next forty-nine years?" He picked up a pebble. He tossed it gently at a pigeon. The bird flew off.

"First I worked for the Pinkerton Detective Agency," he said. "Then I moved to New York and, shall we say, acquired some wealth trading stocks."

Patrick said, "You knew which companies would be successful. And you got rich."

Eugene nodded. "I kept only the funds I needed to get us home. I gave the rest to charity," he said. "Next I worked in science labs around the city. Then Nikola Tesla came to America in 1884."

"You were aging the whole time," Beth said. "That's why you're so old, and Patrick and I aren't. For us it's been only a few days."

Eugene sighed. "Yes, I am now what might be called elderly," he said. "But I'm still smart enough to help you." He released Beth's hand and patted the computer.

"I knew when and where you were at all times," Eugene said. "I was able to keep the computer charged with an adapter I made. It worked with chemical batteries till electricity power became available. Just this month I was able to get the Imagination Stations working."

Patrick said to Beth, "The Imagination Stations can move around the world. But they can't get to a new time yet. We're stuck in 1923."

"Actually," Eugene said, "they currently can move only through portals I programmed. One of the portals is here on this rooftop."

Beth looked confused. "But you have the computer," she said. "Why do you need Mr. Tesla's help?"

"The machines were severely damaged by lightning. I believe that only Mr. Tesla has the answer to completely fixing the machines," Eugene said. "So I followed him and studied every patent of his. I've re-created all his experiments in his abandoned lab called Wardenclyffe. He never knew."

Suddenly Patrick heard the beating of wings. A pigeon flew down and landed near the ladder. It started cooing.

Beth said, "I recognize that bird. It follows

Mr. Tesla around." She hopped up and went to the edge of the roof. She looked down the ladder.

"It's Mr. Tesla!" Beth said. She folded her arms across her chest. "And I'm sure he heard every word."

Tesla climbed the rest of the way up the ladder. He wore a sheepish expression.

Eugene stood. Patrick could see he had tears in his eyes.

"Mr. Tesla," Eugene said, "it's an honor to meet such an esteemed inventor. I admire nearly every aspect of your work. The Tesla coil is exceedingly clever."

He shuffled toward the scientist. "Please allow me to shake your hand." Eugene politely offered his right hand.

Tesla bowed halfway and put his hands behind his back. "Excuse me," he said. "I cannot shake your hand."

Eugene looked crushed. His mouth opened, but no words came out.

Patrick had never seen Eugene speechless before.

Eugene finally gained some self-control. "Is it because I was spying on you?" he asked.

Beth said, "Oh no. He injured his hands not long ago in a laboratory accident."

Eugene paled. "Do you need a doctor?" he asked Tesla.

Patrick saw Beth wink at Eugene.

Beth added, "Mr. Tesla notes your concern. But he doesn't need anyone to look at it."

Tesla said, "Exactly."

"Wait," Patrick said in a loud, panicked voice. "Something's not right!"

Everyone looked at him.

"If Mr. Tesla is here, who has the car Imagination Station?"

The Helicopter

Eugene gulped. "Allow me to check the computer again," he said. He slowly turned to sit back down on the air-vent hood.

Beth walked beside Eugene to make sure he didn't fall.

Patrick suddenly shouted, "Stop!"

Beth looked away from Eugene to see what was happening.

Tesla was rushing toward the modern Imagination Station. "I don't care about the

Model T time machine," he said. "This one is magnificent!"

"He'll steal it!" Beth shouted.

Tesla opened the door on the side of the machine.

Patrick was rushing toward the machine. But Beth thought he would be too late. Tesla could get in and push the red button.

But then the inventor closed the door and opened it again. Tesla's habit of opening things three times slowed him down.

That gave Patrick enough time to get to the Imagination Station. He reached out to touch Tesla's arm.

Tesla pulled back instantly to avoid being touched. He stepped away from the machine.

Patrick quickly climbed inside and shut the door.

Tesla tried to open the door. It wouldn't budge. He grunted and tried again.

Tesla began pounding on the windshield with his fist. "Let me in!" he shouted.

Beth took Eugene's arm. "Come on, Eugene," she said. "Let's get that machine out of here. Mr. Tesla is too curious."

"Excuse me, but what's going on?"

Beth recognized Gerald Norman's voice. She turned. The older boy had come to the rooftop. He had a sketch pad and pencil with him.

"I've come to make the final drawing of Mr. Tesla's new invention," Gerald said.

"A new invention?" Eugene said. "I must see it!"

Tesla stopped pounding on the Imagination Station. He said, "You want to see my invention?"

Beth said, "Yes, please! Show it to us."

Tesla walked over to the large object covered with a tarp. "Gerald," he said, "come help me remove the cover. We will unveil it together."

Gerald said, "Yes, sir." He moved toward the object.

Beth whispered to Eugene, "Get the Imagination Station away from Mr. Tesla."

Eugene nodded. "I'll go back to Wardenclyffe promptly," he whispered. "The Model T machine must have gone to that portal. I will deal with the thief, whoever it is."

The switch went easily. Tesla began taking the tarp off his invention. Patrick got out of the Imagination Station. Eugene got in. He pushed the red button.

The machine vanished silently.

Patrick and Beth gathered around Tesla and Gerald.

"One, two, three!" Tesla said.

The inventor and Gerald pulled off the tarp.

"Ta-da!" Tesla said.

Beth couldn't believe her eyes. Tesla had built a helicopter. The design was as simple as if it were made from Tinkertoys. There were no doors or windshield. The engine looked similar to the engine of the Model T.

Patrick said, "Wow! That's amazing!"

"It's really light so it can run on electricity," Gerald said.

Tesla looked around. He scowled. "Where is my admirer, Eugene Meltsner?" he asked. "Mr. Latimer said Mr. Meltsner is rich. I want him to invest in my ideas."

Patrick stammered, "Well, he, uh, um . . ."

Gerald was straightforward. "The old man got in the white machine. It vanished."

Beth flushed red. Suddenly she felt guilty.

The inventor narrowed his eyes. "You," he said. He pointed at Beth. "You tricked me again. The time machine is gone, along with my investor. And my hope."

Beth moved toward Tesla. "I'm sorry," she said. "An inventor's life is difficult."

She tried to cheer him up a little. "Tell me about your new and improved helicopter. Or better yet, show us."

Tesla's mood seemed to lighten. His moustache twitched. "Of course," he said. "Have a seat." He motioned with his arm toward the helicopter.

Beth wanted to climb in. But it looked scary. "There are no seat belts," she said.

Tesla smiled, "It's perfectly safe. It's a prototype with a new landing system. It will rise only a few hundred feet."

Beth looked at Patrick. He said, "Why not? At least it doesn't shoot death rays or lightning bolts."

Tesla must have guessed she was hesitant. "Here," he said, "I'll go first." Tesla climbed in and sat on one of the two seats. He offered Beth a hand to help her climb in.

Tesla is offering to hold my hand. It must be important, she thought.

Beth accepted Tesla's hand. He pulled her into the seat.

Suddenly there was a flapping of wings. The pigeon settled on Tesla's shoulder. He said, "Hello, little beauty. I'm going to fly like you!"

Tesla quickly flipped a lever. The helicopter's blades began to spin. They made a chopping noise as they sliced through the air.

Beth felt herself lift. The movement made her stomach flip upside down.

The helicopter rose and rose and rose. The wind made her hair flop with each gust. She looked down. Patrick and Gerald looked tiny.

The bird on Tesla's shoulder flew off.

"You said it didn't go high," Beth shouted. "Let's land."

Tesla grinned. "Hang on!" he shouted. "We're going to Wardenclyffe!"

Wardenclyffe

Patrick watched in disbelief as the helicopter flew away. He didn't know what to do to stop them. Soon Tesla and Beth were too far away to see. He lost sight of them as they flew over a river to the east. He said a prayer asking God to keep Beth safe.

He turned to the boy Tesla had called Gerald. Patrick offered his hand and said, "I'm Patrick. It's nice to meet you."

Gerald gave Patrick a hearty handshake. "Gerald Norman," he said. "Uh . . . ah . . ."

Patrick said, "Yes?"

Gerald took a deep breath. "How did that white machine vanish? Did it truly disappear?"

Patrick shrugged. "I don't know exactly what powers it. I just know how to open the door and turn it on. You'll have to ask Mr. Tesla."

"Why ask Mr. Tesla?" Gerald asked. "He's never built something like that."

Patrick smiled. "In a way he built it in his mind," he said. "He just doesn't know that he knows how everything fits together."

"Like when I learned to read," Gerald said. "I knew all the letter sounds. But I hadn't learned how to put the sounds together."

"That makes sense," Patrick said. "But you'd better not tell anyone what you saw."

Gerald sighed and said, "No one would believe me if I did. They'd just say I'd been around Tesla too long. He's known for exaggerating his inventions."

Patrick looked over the river again. "Mr. Tesla said he was going to Wardenclyffe," he said. "Can I take a bus or a subway to get there?"

Gerald was silent.

"I said, can I take . . ." Patrick said and turned to look back at his new friend.

But Gerald wasn't alone.

Patrick's heart started to race. "Mr. Whittaker!" he cried. The person Patrick least expected but wanted to see more than anyone else was standing on the roof. He was right next to the modern Imagination Station.

"Don't take public transportation," Whit said. "Why don't you just come with me?"

Patrick rushed into Whit's arms. The two friends exchanged a brief hug.

Patrick felt tears of joy trying to spill down his face. But he blinked them away.

"Why were you gone so long?" Patrick asked. "You didn't answer your phone when we needed you."

"Did you truly need me?" Whit asked. "It seems as if you, Beth, and Eugene have been managing just fine. I'm proud of you."

Patrick smiled at Mr. Whittaker.

Mr. Whittaker continued, "But I'm sorry if you've been worried. It sounds as though we have some work to do to set things right."

"Then let's go to Wardenclyffe," Patrick said.

Whit put a hand on his shoulder. He gave

Patrick a reassuring pat. "We'll go in just a minute," Whit said. Then he turned to Gerald.

Gerald was running his hands over the outside of the Imagination Station. "It's so beautiful," he said. "May I take a ride in it?"

Whit leaned over to look Gerald in the eyes. Whit smiled. His eyes twinkled.

"I'm afraid not, Gerald," Whit said. "You've got a birthday party to plan for your grandfather. And tomorrow Mr. Tesla will need you. These last years of his life are going to be difficult for him. He'll need better friends than just the birds."

"I'll help all I can, sir," Gerald said. "My grandfather and I will look out for Mr. Tesla's patents." Gerald offered Whit his hand for a good-bye handshake.

Whit chuckled and shook Gerald's hand. Whit said, "The best adventures are often at home, right where you are."

Whit and Patrick climbed into the Imagination Station.

Whit motioned for Patrick to push the red button.

Patrick felt calm and confident. He trusted the machine now that Whit was there. He knew he wouldn't land in a lightning storm or a tsunami.

He slammed the button with his palm. And suddenly everything went black.

● ● ●

Beth closed her eyes. The wind and dust hurt too much for her to open them. The air pressure was making her cheeks flap. She held on to the helicopter seat. Her fingers ached from holding on so tight.

She peeked with one eye and looked down. The helicopter was above water. She wondered what would happen if it crashed into the river. Would the seat cushion be a flotation device?

She could hear Tesla gasping for breath.

He's pretty old, Beth thought. *What if he has a heart attack? What if I have a heart attack?*

Beth closed her eyes again. They traveled about a half hour across the state of New York. She tried to ignore the cold and wind burning her skin. She ignored the creaking sounds of the helicopter straining against the wind. She prayed and prayed and prayed to God that she wouldn't die.

The helicopter banked. Beth noticed a slight change in the rhythm of the blades. She peeked again.

Tesla was turning a lever. Beth felt the helicopter begin to descend.

They were above an open field near a long, one-story building. A tan sedan was parked near the entrance.

Surely Tesla would land the helicopter now. He would use the new landing gear he had designed.

Panic rose again in her heart. *We're going to land with the new gear that has never been tested!*

Thud!

The helicopter landed with Beth's back parallel to the ground.

The landing jostled Beth. Her teeth clamped shut with the impact. Her head slammed against the back of the seat.

Next the helicopter rolled. Then—*thud*— it flopped forward ninety degrees. Now she was sitting upright. She looked at the mad inventor.

Tesla hadn't fared much better. He was thrown half out of his seat. He was holding on with a leg and one hand.

Patrick was suddenly next to them shouting, "Are you okay? Tell me you're okay!"

Tears of fear streamed down Beth's cheeks. But she said, "Check on Mr. Tesla first."

She watched as Patrick reached up to help Tesla out of his seat. The inventor ignored the offered help. Tesla hopped down by himself and brushed past Patrick. He headed toward the long building.

The windows were covered with black paper. But the front door was open. It was possible to see some inventions inside.

"My lab!" Tesla shouted. "It's been restored just as the old man said!"

"Beth?"

She heard a familiar voice. She whipped around to find its owner.

"Mr. Whittaker!" Beth said. Her tears of fear turned to joy. They ran down her chapped cheeks. "I am so happy to see you."

She looked at Patrick. "And you, too,"
she said. "I was afraid Mr. Tesla and I were
doomed!"

Whit helped her out of her seat.

Beth planted her feet firmly on the dirt. She
had never been so glad to be
on the ground. She hugged
Whit and said, "You were
the one who took the
Model T off the roof."

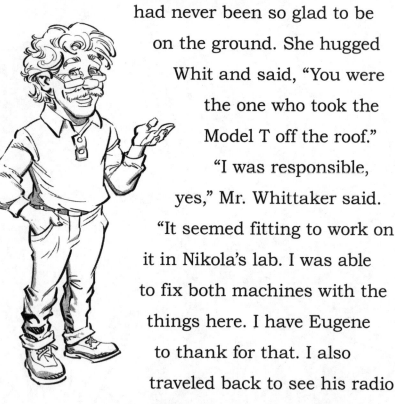

"I was responsible,
yes," Mr. Whittaker said.
"It seemed fitting to work on
it in Nikola's lab. I was able
to fix both machines with the
things here. I have Eugene
to thank for that. I also
traveled back to see his radio
tower, which contained the key for
fixing the time circuits."

Beth wondered what the tower had to do with time travel. But at the moment, she didn't care. She was relieved the machines were working. "May we go home, please?" she asked Whit. "I'd like to visit the good old twenty-first century. I want to be back in Odyssey."

Patrick said, "Soon. But not yet. There's something Mr. Whittaker wants to do in 1923."

Whit smiled. His eyes twinkled with merriment. "Let's all go inside," he said. "There are some people I want you to meet."

Mr. Edison and Mr. Ford

Patrick and Beth walked into the lab. Eugene was asleep in a chair in the corner. Beth was amazed at how fast Tesla recovered from the helicopter flight. He seemed to come alive inside his lab in Wardenclyffe.

Whit had somehow brought in a new, adapted Model T car. Its hood was raised so the engine was exposed. Two men were inspecting it. They had arrived in the fancy tan car outside while Beth was in the helicopter.

Beth and Patrick moved close to the car on display.

Beth whispered to her cousin, "I recognize Mr. Whittaker and Mr. Tesla. But there are two other men in suits and black hats. I'm guessing they're Thomas Edison and Henry Ford. They've been looking to make a better electric car."

"You're right," Patrick said. "Let's edge closer to hear what's going on."

The men were discussing the merits of the Model T's invention.

Beth leaned over to Patrick. She said quietly, "It looks exactly like the engine of the car Imagination Station. But this Model T hasn't been bashed up and cracked. It's a new body. And it has a backseat."

Patrick nodded.

Whit motioned with his hand toward the engine. He spoke to everyone in the room.

"Nikola and I developed an electric engine a

few years ago," he said. "Since then I've been working to perfect this very powerful engine. It's affordable and can easily be reproduced. But we need investors."

Henry Ford spoke up. "Has it been road tested?"

Whit smiled mysteriously. "It's been around the world, so to speak."

Edison said, "I've got my own ideas about improving car batteries. I don't want to invest in something that will replace them. I'll lose money."

Suddenly Tesla blurted out, "But this engine can be used in a time machine! Mr. Whittaker knows how to go back in history!"

Ford merely laughed.

Thomas Edison said, "We don't want to go back in time. That's the difference between you and us, Nikola. We're men of the future!"

This seemed to make Tesla angry. He said, "But you can travel ahead in time too." He turned to Beth and said, "Tell them it's true. Tell them you're from the future."

Beth looked to Whit for the okay. He nodded.

"My cousin and I live in the twenty-first century," she said. "We've got cell phones. I can talk to anyone around the globe." She tried to think of other things to say. "And we have movies and TV, moving pictures in color!"

Patrick added, "And there's this thing called the Internet. It's an electric communication system that unites the world!"

Ford laughed again. "All that tells us is that you kids have seen Nikola's patents. What you're talking about sounds exactly like his wild dreams. He has ideas for all kinds of outlandish inventions that don't work."

Ford turned to Whit. "We need something more practical than an imaginary time machine. We need a better battery."

Edison lifted his hat in a good-bye gesture.

"Thank you for the offer to invest, gentlemen. But we politely say no. I wish you well, Nikola. I hope you find someone who believes in you."

The two famous inventors left.

Beth heard the engine of the fancy sedan roar to life. She went to the lab window and lifted

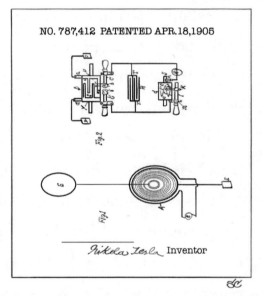

NO. 787,412 PATENTED APR.18,1905

Nikola Tesla Inventor

the black paper. She watched the car drive away.

Eugene woke up and said, "Did I miss anything of great importance?"

He stood and shuffled over next to Nikola

Tesla. Tesla was leaning on the corner of a desk. He looked around at the lab.

"I'm a fool," Tesla said. "No one trusts me. They think I'm a madman."

Tesla pointed to the photo in the newspaper and said, "You came to me for help all those years ago, John Whittaker. And I thought I was so great with my tall transmitter tower. I wouldn't listen to your ideas. They seemed so small at the time." He lowered his head. "I'm sorry."

"I learned a lot from you," Whit said. "After we parted ways, I got the Imagination Station to work after all. And I did consult a few of your patents to do it. They had expired by the time I needed them. But I still owe you a great debt. I'd like to thank you somehow. How would you like to travel to the twenty-first century?"

Tesla's moustache twitched. He asked, "Would you trust me with your machine?"

"Hardly," he said with a laugh. "But there's

a way I can keep you out of trouble. First, Eugene is going with you. Second, the Model T Imagination Station will be in lockdown mode. So you'll be able to see but not get out. And no one will be able to see you."

"What will happen to me?" Eugene asked. "Will I return to my proper age?"

Whit's face turned a bit gray. "I don't know exactly, Eugene," he said. "But we'll deal with that when you return to Odyssey."

Eugene opened his laptop. He typed on the keyboard. The Model T Imagination Station appeared.

Eugene and Tesla got in the car.

Beth saw Tesla turn the steering wheel. There was a flash of colors spinning. And then they disappeared.

Suddenly a bird flew in through the open door of the lab.

"That's Tesla's bird," Beth said. "It follows him everywhere."

She patted the bird's head. "I've got an idea. Let's attach a note to the pigeon. It will fly back to the Hotel Marguery. Tesla will find the message when he gets back!"

"Let's use the telegraph paper," Patrick said. "It's thin." Patrick went to the odd-looking reel machine.

"I know what I want to write," Beth said. She wrote a note on the paper. It said:

Dear Mr. Tesla,

Someday a company that builds electric cars will be named after you. I hope that makes you happy. But you should also look to your past. The best ideas come from the Bible your mom gave you. Don't forget that.

Love, Beth.

Patrick rolled up the message. He found a bit of string and tied it to the bird's leg. He took the pigeon to the door and shooed it away.

Beth said, "Let's go home now."

Patrick said, "One more thing. I'm going to send a telegraph to Mr. Inumaru in Japan. I want him to know why we didn't finish the rice balls."

Beth nodded. "Tell him it was to help Mr. Tesla," she said. "He'll understand."

Whit's End

Patrick and Beth returned to Whit's End in the modern Imagination Station. They were in Whit's workshop. They got out before the machine disappeared. Moments later it came back with Whit.

They all went upstairs to the ice-cream shop. Beth turned on the lights. They flickered a bit.

Beth said, "I hope the storm has finally passed. I don't like being in the dark."

"Look," Patrick said, "there's my backpack. It's right where I left it." It was sitting under one of the small tables. He sighed. "I still have a report to do about the history of soccer."

Whit went to the fountain. He made Patrick and Beth chocolate milkshakes. The cousins sat at the counter, sipping their treats.

"Was Lewis Latimer rich like Edison or poor like Tesla?" Beth asked.

"Well, he wasn't rich," Whit said. "He

was a consultant and draftsman who helped attorneys write good patents. He did invent one important thing—a filament."

Beth swallowed a mouthful of her shake. "What's a filament?" she asked.

"It's part of the lightbulb," Whit said. "Mr. Edison invented the first lightbulb. But Lewis invented an inexpensive filament that made Edison's bulb last longer. Lewis's name is on the patent. But the money went to the company he worked for at the time."

"Did Mr. Latimer read the Bible?" Beth asked.

"We don't know a lot about Mr. Latimer's spiritual life," Whit said. "But we do know some things. He helped start a church in New York City, for example."

"Why do you think Mr. Tesla didn't read the Bible?" Beth said.

"Sometimes scientists focus only on

what they can test and control," Whit said. "And God can't be measured or put into an experiment. He can't be controlled in any way. That frightens some people, even smart scientists."

"What happened to Mr. Latimer's grandson, Gerald Norman?" Patrick asked. "He seemed like a nice kid."

Whit picked up a towel and began to wipe down the counter. "Gerald became a New York judge," Whit said. "His job was to make sure people were paid fairly. Perhaps he did it to help people like his grandfather. Lewis Latimer didn't get paid as much as white men doing the same work."

The cousins were silent as they sipped the rest of their milkshakes. Patrick was still thinking about their last adventure.

Patrick finally said, "I'm still confused about the photo. Mr. Tesla's tower helped you create the Imagination Station, right? So how did you get back there in the first place?"

Beth gasped. "Or are you really from the 1920s?" she asked. "Is Whit's End one of your adventures in the twenty-first century?"

Whit didn't answer. He merely smiled, and his eyes twinkled mysteriously.

To find out more about the next book, *Freedom at the Falls*, visit TheImaginationStation.com.

Secret Word Puzzle

The turn of the twentieth century marked an era of invention. The experiments Nikola Tesla performed startled everyone. His efforts to harness the energy of the world were noble.

Harnessing physical power is good. But did you know that having spiritual power is better? Spiritual power is always available to you. It's enough for everything you need and then some! When you experience spiritual power, it may startle and surprise you.

The Bible talks about good things God will do for us. Those things are often beyond our wildest imaginations!

You can learn more by finding your way out of the maze on the next page. Then copy down the letters in order on the lines and in the boxes. When you finish, you'll know all of Ephesians 3:20. The word in the box is the secret word.

"Now to him who is able to do far more abundantly than all that we ask or think, according to the . . .

P o w e r at w _ _ _

_ _ _ _ _ _ _."

Secret Word Puzzle

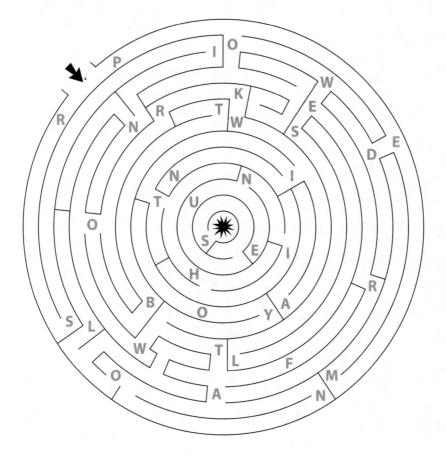

THE IMAGINATION STATION

FOCUS ON THE FAMILY PRESENTS

THE KEY TO ADVENTURE LIES WITHIN YOUR IMAGINATION.

1 VOYAGE WITH THE VIKINGS
2 ATTACK AT THE ARENA
3 PERIL IN THE PALACE
4 REVENGE OF THE RED KNIGHT
5 SHOWDOWN WITH THE SHEPHERD
6 PROBLEMS IN PLYMOUTH
7 SECRET OF THE PRINCE'S TOMB
8 BATTLE FOR CANNIBAL ISLAND
9 ESCAPE TO THE HIDING PLACE
10 CHALLENGE ON THE HILL OF FIRE
11 HUNT FOR THE DEVIL'S DRAGON
12 DANGER ON A SILENT NIGHT
13 THE REDCOATS ARE COMING!
14 CAPTURED ON THE HIGH SEAS
15 SURPRISE AT YORKTOWN
16 DOOMSDAY IN POMPEII
17 IN FEAR OF THE SPEAR
18 TROUBLE ON THE ORPHAN TRAIN
19 LIGHT IN THE LIONS' DEN
20 INFERNO IN TOKYO

OVER **750,000** SOLD IN SERIES

.... COLLECT ALL OF THEM TODAY! ....

AVAILABLE AT A CHRISTIAN RETAILER NEAR YOU